Pearlie and the Silver Fern Fairy

WENDY HARMER

Illustrated by Gypsy Taylor

RANDOM HOUSE AUSTRALIA

For Shirley, our own precious Kiwi.

A Random House book
Published by Random House Australia Pty Ltd
Level 3, 100 Pacific Highway, North Sydney NSW 2060
www.randomhouse.com.au

First published by Random House Australia in 2011
Copyright © Out of Harms Way Pty Ltd 2011

Addresses for companies within the Random House Group can be found
at www.randomhouse.com.au/offices.
National Library of Australia

Cataloguing-in-Publication Entry
    Harmer, Wendy
    Pearlie and the Silver Fern Fairy / Wendy Harmer; illustrator Gypsy Taylor
    ISBN 978 1 74166 379 2 (pbk.)
    Series: Harmer, Wendy. Pearlie the park fairy; 13
    Target audience: For children
    Subjects: Fairies – Juvenile fiction
    Other authors/contributors: Taylor, Gypsy

    A823.3

Designed and typeset by Jobi Murphy
Printed and bound by Sing Cheong Printing Co. Ltd, Hong Kong
10 9 8 7 6 5 4 3 2 1

Pearlie the Park Fairy flew through a long, white cloud. Below her was the beautiful country of New Zealand.

Riding on the back of Queen Emerald's magic ladybird, Pearlie saw huge snowy mountains, shimmering lakes and a mighty green rainforest.

The ladybird flew lower through the towering trees and set Pearlie down on a mossy rock, then it winked and whizzed off. It was a cool misty morning and Pearlie wrapped a warm coat over her wings.

'Hurly-burly!' she said. 'I've never seen a park like this before.'

Pearlie heard a voice tinkling like a silver bell. She darted to the bank of a rushing stream and there was a beautiful fairy riding in a little canoe made from a seed pod. The fairy was wearing a long, feathery cloak.

She smiled and waved to Pearlie. *'Kia ora! Welcome! Jump in and start paddling.'*

Pearlie thought it was rather curious that they were taking a canoe instead of flying, but she leapt in and off they sailed.

'My name is Omaka,' said the fairy. 'In Māori talk that means "place where the stream flows".'

'Are you a park fairy too?' asked Pearlie.

'Āe mārika! Yes, indeed!' smiled Omaka. 'But we're a long way from the city here in the ancient rainforest. This is a park for nature at its wild and most beautiful best.'

The little canoe slipped downstream around rocks and under low branches. The sunlight sparkled on the damp fern fronds, turning them silver.

Pearlie thought she'd never seen a sight so lovely.

Soon the bubbling stream joined another that was moving more swiftly. Pearlie looked up in alarm. Ahead was a waterfall tumbling down a rocky cliff. The little canoe was heading straight for the swirling water!

'Reeds and ripples!' cried Pearlie.

'Hold on. Paddle harder!' called Omaka.

The canoe twirled and danced and swayed on the water. Then, with barely a splash, it sailed right through the waterfall and beyond, into a cave twinkling with lights.

'Ooooh, stars and moonbeams!' said Pearlie.

'No, they're glow-worms,' laughed Omaka.
'They're showing us the way to my place.'

Before long, the fairies were sitting on gleaming paua shells in Omaka's cosy cave house and sipping on snowberry tea.

'It was a good day to come,' said Omaka. 'I'm planning a little birthday supper for my friend tonight, and you'll be able to meet everyone. I have to bake the cake and deliver these invitations.'

'I'd be glad to help,' said Pearlie.

'*Ka pai!* Excellent!' said Omaka. 'I've put a list of the guests and a map of where to find them in this bag.'

Pearlie took the small woven bag and slung it over her shoulder. 'And who is celebrating their birthday?' she asked.

'My friend the tuatara,' Omaka smiled. Pearlie had never heard of such a creature. 'He's one hundred and fifty years old today.'

'One hundred and fifty years old!' Pearlie gasped.

'Yes! That's a lot of candles and a very big cake, so I'd better get started,' said Omaka. 'And so had you, Pearlie. *Mā te wā*. See you later.'

Pearlie climbed back in the canoe and set off.
The paddling made her very warm and she took
off her coat. Her silvery wings fluttered free.

Pearlie followed the map deep into the rainforest. She tied the canoe to a reed and read the name on the first invitation. It was 'Colin the kiwi'.

'Roots and twigs! What's a kiwi?' wondered Pearlie.

She flitted off and quickly spotted a small brown hairy bundle sitting in a hole in the ground.

Pearlie flew down and saw two bright eyes
staring at her through bristling whiskers at the
top of a long, narrow beak. So a kiwi was a
very large bird!

'How do you do, Colin?' said Pearlie politely.
'Here's a party invitation for you.'

'Wonderful,' Colin snorted happily.

'If you could fly by at sunset, that would be perfect,' said Pearlie.

'Well, of course I can't fly, but I'll wander along just the same,' he said. '*Tēnā koe*. Thank you!'

Pearlie was puzzled. A bird that couldn't fly? She didn't want to be rude and ask what was wrong with his wings, so she simply thanked Colin and flew off.

The next invitation was for 'Hoki the kakapo'.

'Oh dear,' said Pearlie. 'I've never heard of a kakapo either.' Was it a fish or a frog, or another odd kind of creature, she wondered.

Just where the map said, Pearlie spied a big lump covered in glorious green feathers snoozing under a tree fern.

So a kakapo was a bird too!

It was much bigger than the kiwi. In fact, it was the most enormous parrot Pearlie had ever seen. She gently woke Hoki and handed over the invitation.

'Please fly by later for some cake,' she said.

'Well, I've never been one for flying,' yawned Hoki as he fluffed his feathers. 'But I do love cake, so I'll hike along the trail and see you there.'

Now Pearlie was a little worried. Another bird that wouldn't fly? Why ever not? She fluttered lower than before, just to be careful. This was a strange part of the world indeed!

Now Pearlie had one last invitation to deliver, for 'Wanda the short-tailed bat'.

'Well, at least I know what a bat is,' said Pearlie as she flew along. 'She will be hanging upside down in this tree here.'

But there was no bat in the branches.

Then Pearlie saw something moving down on the forest floor. A small snout was poking out from under a leaf. Pearlie's wings flashed as she zoomed down.

'Wanda?' asked Pearlie. 'Is that you?'

The leaf stirred and out came a tiny snuffling bat.

'Āna. It's me,' said Wanda.

Pearlie gave her the invitation. 'Just fly on over
when the sun has gone down.'

I'd rather stroll by, if it's all the same to you,
said Wanda.

'Why, yes, of course,' said Pearlie kindly, even
though by now she was beginning to feel rather
nervous. She looked towards the treetops. Why
was nobody flying?

Pearlie ran off through the forest as fast as she could. She didn't dare use her wings. There must be something up in the sky that would catch any creature that flew. Maybe it would eat her!

The sun was fading and scary shadows crowded the forest. Pearlie found a hollow in the roots of a tree and huddled there for a moment. Her tiny heart was beating fast.

'Beaks and claws!' said Pearlie. 'I'd better be careful and walk back to Omaka's place, even though it will take me ages. And . . . brrr,' She shivered. 'It's getting c-c-cold.' She pulled her coat over her shoulders.

Suddenly a huge head topped with fearsome spikes poked itself in front of Pearlie's face. Two great black eyes stared at her!

'Eeeek!' she cried. 'Don't eat me! Please, don't eat me!'

Pearlie felt for her wand and then remembered she had left it behind in the glow-worm cave.

The scaly beast opened its mouth wide. Surely it would eat Pearlie with one mighty gulp!

Then the great mouth smiled.

'Heh, heh! Don't be frightened, little one. I'm Grandfather Tuatara. Can I offer you a lift to Omaka's cave? It's my birthday today and I hear there will be cake!'

Pearlie laughed with surprise. 'You're a lizard,' she said.

'*Nāhea!* Not me!' chuckled Grandfather Tuatara. 'I come from the dinosaurs who roamed the earth 200 million years ago. This is the only place on earth you can find me. Climb up and I'll tell you a few stories along the way. Watch out though, my name means "peaks on the back" in Māori.'

Pearlie scrambled aboard, minding the spikes on Grandfather's back, and they set off. No one in Jubilee Park would ever believe she'd ridden a dinosaur!

As they rambled along, crunching over carpets of leaves and ducking under dripping fern fronds, Grandfather Tuatara told Pearlie many tales of ancient days. He pointed out tiny flowers, plants and moss on the forest floor. Walking was a good way to see them all.

'There are so many creatures here that don't fly. Why is that, Grandfather?' asked Pearlie.

'Well, long ago, the forest was safe and we had no need to fly, so many creatures never learned how,' Grandfather explained as he trudged along on sturdy legs. 'But since then many things have come across the ocean that can hunt and hurt us. Humans brought creatures with sharp teeth – rats and cats, dogs and possums, weasels, stoats and ferrets. We couldn't fly away to escape. In my time I have seen so many good friends disappear,' he sighed sadly.

Pearlie was quiet, thinking about all the poor creatures in danger. What would happen if the fairies were to disappear too?

'We hope for better times,' said Grandfather.
'I know that young humans care about
us and that's a very good thing.'

'It is,' Pearlie agreed.

'Rā whānau ki a koe!
Happy birthday to you!'

Grandfather Tuatara stopped in his tracks. In a clearing were all his friends – Omaka, Colin, Hoki and Wanda – and in the middle was a tremendous birthday cake with one hundred and fifty candles.

Pearlie leapt from Grandfather's back. As she jumped, her coat fell off.

It was then that Omaka spied Pearlie's beautiful wings. 'You can fly!' she cried.

Pearlie was astonished to see that Omaka had no wings at all.

A fairy that couldn't fly? She was just as precious as all the other creatures of the ancient rainforest.

'Can you light Grandfather's candles for us?' asked Omaka, as she gave Pearlie her wand.

'Of course!' said Pearlie. She whizzed around the cake, lighting all the candles in a blinding flash.

Grandfather Tuatara took a deep breath and blew them all out.

'We have a present for you, Pearlie,' said
Omaka. 'It's a koru carved from greenstone.
It is the shape of a new fern frond, which brings
new life and hope. Wear it to keep you strong.'

'I will keep it forever,' said Pearlie.
'And I hope all my friends in the
rainforest will live in peace.'

'*Ehara ehara*, indeed,' said
Grandfather. 'Now it's
time for cake!'

Soon the bubbling stream joined another that was moving more swiftly. Pearlie looked up in alarm. Ahead was a waterfall tumbling down a rocky cliff. The little canoe was heading straight for the swirling water!

'Reeds and ripples!' cried Pearlie.

'Hold on. Paddle harder!' called Omaka.